World of Fairy Tales

Sleeping Beauty
and
Snow White and the Seven Dwarfs

Two Tales and Their Histories

alphabet
soup

an imprint of

WINDMILL
BOOKS
New York

Published in 2010 by Windmill Books, LLC
303 Park Avenue South, Suite # 1280, New York, NY 10010-3657

Adaptations to North American Edition © 2010 Windmill Books

Editor (Arcturus): Carron Brown
Designer: Steve Flight

Library of Congress Cataloging-in-Publication Data

Brown, Carron.
  Sleeping Beauty and Snow White and the seven dwarfs : two tales and their histories / Carron
Brown.— 1st North American ed.
      p. cm.— (World of fairy tales)
Summary: A retelling, accompanied by a brief history, of the two well-known tales in the first of
which a fairy's curse causes a young princess to sleep for 100 years and, in the second, a
beautiful princess finds refuge from her wicked stepmother in the forest home of the seven
dwarves.
  ISBN 978-1-60754-634-4 (library binding)—ISBN 978-1-60754-635-1 (pbk.)
  ISBN 978-1-60754-636-8 (6-pack)
  1. Fairy tales. [1. Fairy tales. 2. Folklore—Germany.] I. Sleeping Beauty. II. Snow White and
the seven dwarfs. English. III. Title. IV. Title: Sleeping Beauty and Snow White. V. Title: Snow
White and the seven dwarfs.
  PZ8.B697Sle 2010
  [398.2]—dc22

                          2009037521

Printed in China

CPSIA Compliance Information: Batch #AW0102W: For further information contact Windmill Books, New York, New York at 1-866-478-0556.

For more great fiction and nonfiction, go to windmillbooks.com.

Sleeping Beauty

ONCE UPON A TIME, THERE WAS A KING AND A
queen who had no children. This made them very sad. One day,
the queen bathed in the pond near the castle. The sky was bright,
the birds were singing, but the queen was sad. She sighed.

"Oh, how I'd love to have a child!"

Suddenly, a frog sitting on a lily pad answered her:

"In a year and a day, you will have a child."

Then the frog disappeared at once.

3

After the year, the frog's prediction came true. The queen gave birth to a
lovely little girl. The king and queen decided to give a christening party
and invited the seven fairies of their kingdom to be the child's godmothers.
Each fairy was to give the princess a gift. All the important people in the
kingdom were also invited to come to the party.

After the christening, all the guests were led into the hall where a feast
was given in honor of the fairy godmothers. Each of their places was laid
with beautiful golden plates and cutlery encrusted with diamonds and rubies.
Everyone sat down at the huge table. After the feast, each of the fairies went
up to the little princess's cradle to give her a gift.

The first fairy gave her beauty, the second gave her
grace, and the third gave her intelligence. The next three gave
her the gift of dancing gracefully, singing like a nightingale, and
playing all musical instruments wonderfully. But at that moment a harsh
voice shrilled out, making them all shiver. A dark shape entered the room.
It was a very ugly and evil fairy, who the king and queen had not invited.
They had thought she was dead or locked up in a tower.

"Hee! Hee!" she cackled. "You didn't invite me. I have come to bring
the princess a gift. And here it is: one day she will prick her finger with
the spindle on a spinning wheel and she will die! Hee! Hee! Hee!"

5

Frozen with horror, the guests stood speechless and frightened. At that moment, the youngest and prettiest of the fairies came forward. She had been hiding behind a tapestry in order to speak last, in case an evil gift was given to the princess. She had not yet spoken, so she said:

"King and queen, set your minds at ease. The princess will *not* die. I have no power to undo the old fairy's spell. The princess will prick herself with a spindle, but she will not die. She will fall asleep for a hundred years until a handsome prince comes to wake her."

Immediately, the king
passed a law forbidding anyone
in the kingdom to spin with a
spindle or to own a spinning wheel.

7

A few years later, as the fairies had foretold, the princess grew into a wonderful young woman and was loved by everyone.

One day, the king and the queen were called away on urgent business. The young princess was left alone and wandered from room to room. Suddenly, she discovered a staircase leading up to the castle tower. She went up the stairs and found herself in a dark little room, where an old woman was sitting at a spinning wheel.

"What's that?" the princess asked the old woman.

"It's a spinning wheel, my child. It's to spin wool," answered the old woman.

"Can I try it?"

"Of course, my child, every girl should learn to spin."

Hardly had the princess sat down when she accidentally pricked her finger on the spindle. Immediately, the princess cried out and fainted. The old woman disappeared in an instant with an evil cackle.

At the very moment when the princess fainted, every creature in the castle fell into a deep sleep: the king and queen fell asleep on their thrones, the ladies in waiting fell asleep where they stood, as did the guards and soldiers, leaning on their swords and lances. Lucette, the princess's little dog, and all the horses in the stables also fell asleep.

There was absolute silence everywhere. Suddenly, thousands of trees, bushes, and thorns sprang up around the castle. The vegetation grew so quickly that soon the castle's high towers were almost hidden by it. Not even a mouse could have gotten through the thick, thorny hedge to disturb the sleep of those inside.

A hundred years later, a king's
son from a neighboring country, was
hunting near the castle when he suddenly
saw the towers peeping out from above the thick
tangle of bushes. He had heard that an ogre lived there
or that sorcerers met there at night. But an old peasant
told him the story of the sleeping princess and the prince
who was to save her. The prince did not hesitate: he
galloped towards the castle. Bushes came at him,
scratching and strangling him. Slashing at them with
his sword, he forced his way through. Suddenly, the
trees and thorns parted, as if by enchantment, and
the prince rode up to the castle along a wide path.

11

A deathly hush
hung over the castle
courtyard. The prince came
across the sleeping guards.
and wondered if there
were others in the castle
who were also in
a deep sleep.

12

Intrigued, the prince entered the throne room and was surprised to see that the king, the queen, and their subjects were indeed fast asleep. He went through all the rooms in the castle. Finally, he came to the staircase up to the castle tower and climbed up eagerly. He came into a golden room and discovered the most marvelous sight he had ever seen.

The beautiful princess lay on her bed: she was very still and her face
shone with peace and beauty. The prince knelt down. Trembling, he
bent over her and gently kissed her delicate brow. The princess
moved, looked at him in surprise and exclaimed:

"Is it you, my prince? You've kept me waiting a long time..."

14

The prince was thrilled to hear these words and immediately fell in love with the princess. He took her in his arms and asked her to marry him. The princess looked straight into his eyes and accepted at once.

Meanwhile, the whole castle awoke from sleep. The king picked up the conversation with the queen where he had left off. Respectfully, the guards and soldiers stood back to attention. The princess's little dog began to bark and the horses in the stables began to neigh. The princess came down from the castle tower on the arm of her prince and presented him to her parents.

Quickly, the king and queen ordered the wedding to be celebrated
throughout the kingdom. The prince and princess lived happily
ever after. They had lots of children and often told them the
story of Sleeping Beauty.

THE END

Snow White and the Seven Dwarfs

ONCE UPON A TIME, IN THE HEART OF WINTER, IN A
faraway kingdom, a queen sat sewing by a window. The window
frame was deep black. As she watched the snowflakes falling, she
pricked herself with her needle and three drops of blood fell onto the snow.
"Ah," said the queen with a sigh, "if only I could have a child with hair
as black as ebony, a mouth as red as blood, and skin as white as snow."
Not long after, the queen's wish was granted, and she gave birth to
a girl with hair as black as ebony, a mouth as red as blood, and
skin as white as snow. She called her Snow White.

But not long after the child's birth, the queen fell ill and died. The king
married again. His bride was a very beautiful woman, but so proud and
jealous that she could not bear any woman more beautiful than herself.
The new queen had a magic mirror, which she questioned every day:

"Mirror, mirror on the wall,
Who is the fairest of them all?" she asked it.
And the mirror answered:
"Your Majesty, there's no doubt at all:
You are the fairest of them all!"

Years passed, and Snow White grew more beautiful every day. The queen kept asking her mirror who was the most beautiful. One day the magic mirror answered:

"Your Majesty, you are fair, it's true,
But Snow White is far fairer than you."

The queen knew that Snow White had become more beautiful than she was. Crazy with jealousy, she sent for a hunter and told him:

"Take Snow White into the forest and kill her. Bring me back her liver and her lungs. Then I will know that Snow White is dead!"

The hunter took Snow White into the forest. But when he raised his great knife to kill her, the girl began to cry:

"I beg you, let me live. I will run into the forest and never come back. The queen will never know," she pleaded.

The hunter took pity on Snow White and let her run away. He caught and killed a young deer in her place and took back its liver and lungs to the queen to prove that he had obeyed her. She had them cooked with salt and ate them.

Meanwhile, the terrified Snow White ran through the forest. She scratched herself on thorns and saw wild beasts jump out in front of her. They brushed against her but did her no harm. Eventually, night began to fall and Snow White grew very tired.

Suddenly, she saw a little house in a clearing. The door was open so she went in. Inside, everything was so small that it was like a dolls' house. In the middle of the room stood a little table with a pretty white cloth. On the tablecloth, there were seven little plates, with seven little spoons, seven little knives, seven little forks, and seven little goblets. Along the wall stood a row of seven tiny beds.

Snow White was very hungry and thirsty. She ate a little from each of the seven little plates and drank from each of the seven little goblets. Then she felt so tired that she wanted to lie down. She tried each of the little beds, one after the other, but none of them fit her. In the end she fell asleep curled up in the last one because she was so tired.

It was night when the owners of the little house came home.
They were seven dwarfs, who worked every day at digging
in the mountain to find a bit of gold and a few precious stones.
When they got home, they lit their seven little candles.

Then they saw that someone had come into their house while they were working.

"Who's been sitting on my chair?" asked the first.

"Who's been eating from my plate?" asked the second.

"Who's been taking my bread?" asked the third.

"Who's been eating my vegetables?" asked the fourth.

"Who's been using my fork?" asked the fifth.

"Who's been cutting with my knife?" asked the sixth.

"Who's been drinking from my goblet?" asked the seventh.

The first dwarf turned towards his bed and saw that his bedding was rumpled.

"Who's been lying in my bed?" he cried.

Soon the others ran up and they all shouted together:

"Someone's been lying in my bed too!"

Then the seventh dwarf found Snow White,
fast asleep in his bed. He called his friends,
who rushed up and shouted with surprise.
They all went to fetch their little candles and
stood in a circle around the bed.

"Oh! How beautiful she is!" they cried.

The seven dwarfs did not have the heart to wake
Snow White. The seventh dwarf went to sleep with
the others and spent an hour in each of their beds.

Morning came, and Snow White woke up. When she saw the seven dwarfs, she was very frightened. But they asked her kindly:

"What is your name?"

"My name is Snow White," she replied.

She told how the queen had tried to kill her, how the hunter had disobeyed, and how she had run all day before she found the house. The seven dwarfs said to her:

"If you would like to keep house for us, do the cooking, make the beds, do the washing and mending, you can stay with us. You will never want for anything." Snow White found the seven dwarfs so friendly that she accepted. So she settled into the little house. Every day, while the seven dwarfs were working down the mine, she did the housework. When they came home, dinner was always ready. Since she was alone all day, the kind little dwarfs warned her to be very careful:

"Take care, Snow White!" they said. "Don't let anyone in."

Meanwhile, the queen in her palace thought that she was once again the most beautiful woman of all. So she sat in front of her magic mirror and asked:

"Mirror, mirror on the wall,

Who is the fairest of them all?"

But the mirror answered:

"Your Majesty, you are fair, 'tis true,

But over steep mountain fell,

Where the seven dwarfs dwell,

Snow White is far fairer than you!"

Crazy with jealousy, the wicked woman thought for a long time how she could destroy Snow White forever. Since she was also a witch, she shut herself up in her laboratory. There she created a terrible poison apple, which was red on one side and green on the other. It was so fine and shiny that no one could resist the urge to take a bite from it.

But the red half was poisoned, while the green half was harmless. Then the wicked queen dressed and made herself up to look like a poor old woman. In this disguise, she went to the home of the seven dwarfs. When she came to the house, she knocked on the door and called:

"I have fine apples to sell!"

Snow White looked out of the window and replied:

"I am not allowed to let anyone in. The seven dwarfs have forbidden me."

"But you can have a look," said the fake apple seller. "Do you see this beautiful apple? It's the only one I have left; I have not managed to sell it. I'll tell you what— let's share it. I'll let you have the best part, the red part, and I'll eat the green part."

When she saw the old woman biting so heartily into her half of the apple, Snow White could not resist. She took the other half—the poisoned half—and ate it. No sooner had she bitten off a mouthful than she fell down dead.

Satisfied, the queen gave a cruel cackle and ran off.

When evening came, the seven dwarfs came home and saw Snow White lying on the floor. She was not breathing. They tried everything they could to wake her up, but it was no good.

The dwarfs realized that she was truly dead. They wept for three whole days. Then they decided to bury her. But she was so fresh and lovely that she seemed to be still alive.

"We can't bury her like that in the earth," they said.

So they made her a clear glass coffin. They laid her in it and decorated the lid with her name in big golden letters. Then they took it to the top of the mountain and took turns watching over her. Every day wild animals came with them to weep for the girl.

One fine day, a prince who was riding up the mountain saw Snow White in her coffin. He found her so beautiful that he fell desperately in love.

"Let me take away the coffin," he said to the seven dwarfs. "I'll give you anything you want!"

At first, the dwarfs refused. Then they told him the whole story of Snow White. And they were so moved by the prince's distress that they agreed to let him take away their friend. So the prince ordered his servants to carry off the precious load. They lifted the coffin onto their shoulders and set out. Suddenly, one of them stumbled. Snow White had been roughly shaken, and this dislodged the mouthful of poisoned apple she had eaten. She opened her eyes, lifted the glass coffin lid and asked:

"Where am I?"

The prince told her what had happened and asked her to marry him. Charmed by him and grateful to him for saving her, Snow White accepted at once. He took her to his castle and preparations were made for the wedding. The evil queen was invited too. Before leaving for the wedding, she asked her mirror:

"Mirror, mirror on the wall,

Who is the fairest of them all?"

And the mirror answered:

"Your Majesty, you are fair, 'tis true,

But the princess to be is far fairer than you."

Angry and curious, the queen set out for the wedding. When she arrived at the castle and recognized her stepdaughter, who was about to become the prince's bride, she was speechless with terror. To punish her, the seven dwarfs made her dance on burning coals until she died.

As for Snow White, she lived happily ever after with her prince and had many, many children.

THE END

History of Sleeping Beauty

"Sleeping Beauty" is a tale that has been told for centuries. A version of the story appeared in 12th century Norse mythology in which the god Odin becomes angry with the valkyrie Brunhilda and curses her to sleep until someone rescues and marries her.

Five hundred years later, in 1634, a fairy tale called "Sun, Moon and Talia" was written by an Italian named Giambattista Basile. He based his stories on tales that were not written down, but were remembered and spoken. This way of telling tales is called oral traditions. In Basile's story, Beauty is called Talia and evil is represented by a group of wise men. A married king has two children with Talia, which his wife, the queen, orders to be cooked for dinner. Talia pricks her finger with a splinter of thread and falls into a dead sleep. When she wakes up, the queen tries to kill her, but the king comes to her rescue. He is then told by the queen that he has eaten his children, but the cook admits that he's actually hidden the king's son and daughter and they are well. The queen is killed and the king marries Talia—they live together happily with their children.

A French author, Charles Perrault, published his version of the story as "Sleeping Beauty" over sixty years later, in 1697. The evil fairy makes her appearance for the first time and delivers a curse on Beauty. The story then follows the same tale as Basile's story, except that the king is a prince and the queen is the prince's mother.

In the early 1800s, German folklorists the Brothers Grimm published their version of the story as "Little Briar Rose," and it is their nicer tale that is told today, with the prince waking Rose (Beauty) with a kiss.

The moral of the story is that good things come to those who wait and people shouldn't rush into things, but think carefully about what they plan to do. Sleeping Beauty rushed into the tower and, without thinking, tried the spinning wheel, and so she came to harm. After a long wait, she meets her prince and lives happily ever after.

History of Snow White and the Seven Dwarfs

This tale was well known around Europe and even in Africa and Asia for centuries before it was ever written down. The first detailed European collection of fairy tales, *Il Pentamerone* by the Italian poet Giambattista Basile, was published in 1634—36. It contains the earliest written-down version of the tale, which is called "The Young Slave." In this story, the beautiful girl is called Lisa; she is cursed by a fairy and she falls into a deathly sleep when she is seven years old. Her mother places her in a crystal coffin and hides her in a palace. But when her mother dies, her evil aunt finds the beautiful girl asleep in the crystal box and pulls her out. By doing so, the curse is broken and the girl wakes up only to be made into a slave at the palace by her aunt, who is jealous of Lisa's beauty. Finally, her uncle discovers that the slave is his niece and rescues her.

The famous version of the tale was written by the German authors, the Brothers Grimm, after they heard the story from two sisters who lived in the German town of Cassel. In the first version of the story, it was Snow White's mother who wanted her dead and it is Snow White's father who finds her in her death sleep and rescues her. The stepmother was added by the brothers in a later printing of the story.

In other versions of the tale, the dwarf characters are robbers and the magic mirror is the sun or the moon. There is even a version of the story from Albania published in 1864 that has the beautiful girl living with 40 dragons.

The seven dwarfs are not named in any of the older versions of the tale. It was only when the first movie version *Snow White and the Seven Dwarfs* was released by Walt Disney in 1937 that the dwarfs were each given a name.

The moral of the Snow White story is that jealousy cannot lead to good things, for the evil queen was jealous of Snow White's beauty and it was she and not Snow White who had the unhappy ending.